COBWEB CHRISTMAS

story by
SHIRLEY CLIMO

illustrations by
JANE MANNING

Revised and newly illustrated edition

HARPERCOLLINSPUBLISHERS

Cobweb Christmas

A revised and newly illustrated edition of The Cobweb Christmas, published by Harper and Row 1982.   Text copyright © 1982, 2001 by Shirley Climo
Illustrations copyright © 2001 by Jane Manning   Printed in the U.S.A. All rights reserved.   www.harperchildrens.com   Library of Congress Cataloging-in-Publication Data
Climo, Shirley.   Cobweb Christmas / story by Shirley Climo ;   illustrations by Jane Manning.   p.   cm   Summary: Long ago in Germany, an old woman cleans her house
and decorates her Christmas tree, hoping that this year she will witness some special Christmas Eve magic.   ISBN 0-06-029033-1 — ISBN 0-06-029034-X (lib. bdg.)
[1. Christmas—Fiction.   2. Christmas tree—Fiction.   3. Magic—Fiction.   4. Spider webs—Fiction.   5. Germany—Fiction.]
I. Manning, Jane K., ill.   II. Title.   PZ7.C62247 Co 2000   [E]—dc21   00-047955   CIP   AC
Typography by Carla Weise   1 2 3 4 5 6 7 8 9 10   ❖   First Edition

To my children,
to their children,
and to all their animals
—S.C.

To Anne H.
For her inspiration
and friendship
—J.M.

Once upon a Christmastime, long ago in Germany, there was a little old woman. She was so little she had to stand on a stool to climb into bed and so old she couldn't even count all the Christmases she'd seen. The children in the nearby village called her *Tante*, which means "Auntie" in German.

Tante lived at the edge of a pine forest in a tiny cottage just large enough for her to keep a canary for singing, a cat for purring, and a dog to lie beside the fire.

Squeezed up against the cottage was a barn. In it Tante kept a donkey for riding and a goat for milk and cheese. She had a noisy rooster to wake her in the morning and a speckled hen to lay an egg for her breakfast.

With so many animals about, her little cottage wasn't very tidy, but a bit of fur, a few feathers, or a spiderweb or two didn't bother Tante. Except once a year, when the days got short and the nights grew long, the old lady would nod her head and say, "Time to clean for Christmas."

Then Tante shook the quilt and scoured the kettle until it shone. She scrubbed the

floor on her hands and knees and stood
tiptoe on her stool to sweep the cobwebs
from the rafters.

"Shoo!" said Tante. She swished her
broom and sent every spider and each wisp
of web flying out the door.

When she'd cleaned her home from
corner to corner, the little old woman nodded
and said, "Time to fetch Christmas."

Tante took an ax from the barn and hung the harness with bells on the donkey. She scrambled onto his back, and they trotted into the forest. They circled round and round until the old lady cried, "There!" She pointed to a pine tree no bigger than she was. "That one's just right," she told the donkey.

Tante chopped down the tree, taking care to leave a bough behind so it might grow again. Then, bells jingling, they went home, only now the donkey carried the tree upon his back, and Tante skipped along beside him.

The tree fit perfectly in the tiny cottage. The old woman nodded and said, "Time to make Christmas."

Tante made cookies for the tree. She baked gingerbread boys and girls. She rolled sugar cookies shaped like new moons and cut cinnamon-cookie stars. She rubbed

apples until they gleamed like glass to hang from the
branches, too. Next she put a red ribbon on a bone for the
dog and tied a sprig of catnip for the cat. Tante scattered
corn for the chickens and seeds for the canary, and she
heaped oats in a basket for the donkey and goat.

Then the old woman nodded and said, "Time to share Christmas."
Each year, Tante invited the village children to come and see her tree.
"Tante!" they shouted. "It's the most wonderful tree in the world."
"Tell me if it tastes as good as it looks," she said.

After the children nibbled the apples and the cookies, and ate every crumb of gingerbread, they hurried home to put their shoes by their doors for Kriss Kringle. He was the Christmas visitor who went from house to house tucking gifts into waiting shoes.

Then Tante asked the
animals to share Christmas.

The dog, the cat, the
canary, the hen, the rooster,
and some small shy wild
creatures crowded around
the tree. The donkey and the
goat peered in the doorway.
Tante had something for
everyone—everyone except
the spiders, for they'd all
been brushed away.

But no one could give
the little old lady what she
wanted.

All her life, Tante had heard tales about marvelous happenings on Christmas Eve. Animals might speak aloud. Bees might hum carols, or cocks crow at midnight. Tante wished she could witness a bit of Christmas magic, too.

She sighed and sat down in her rocking chair. "Time to wait for Christmas," said the old lady, and she nodded and nodded her head.

Tante was so tired from cleaning and cooking that she fell fast asleep. She did not know if the rooster crowed when the clock struck twelve or if the dog whispered secrets to the cat. And she did not hear the squeaky voices calling at her door, "Let us in!"

Someone else heard.

Kriss Kringle was passing the cottage on his way to take toys to the village children. He stopped to listen and saw hundreds of spiders on Tante's doorstep.

"We have never shared a Christmas," the biggest spider explained. "Each year Tante sweeps us away. Please, Kriss Kringle, would you let us see Tante's tree?"

Kriss Kringle looked down at the spiders. "There's no harm in that," he said. Before he went on to the village, he opened Tante's door a crack.

Huge spiders, tiny spiders, smooth spiders, hairy spiders, spotted spiders, striped spiders, brown and black and yellow spiders, and the palest kind of see-through spiders came *creeping, crawling, sneaking softly, scurrying, hurrying, quickly, lightly, zigging, zagging, weaving, and wobbling* into the old woman's cottage.

The curious spiders crept closer and closer to Tante's tree. One, two, three skittered up the trunk, and all the other spiders followed.

Silently they ran from branch to branch, back and forth, up and down the tree. Wherever the spiders went, they left a trail behind. Threads looped from limb to limb, and webs were woven everywhere.

Now the busy little spiders had shared Christmas. They had seen and felt every twig on the tree, so they scuttled away.

When he had put a gift in all the children's shoes, Kriss Kringle returned to latch Tante's door. He peeked inside and discovered her tree tangled with sticky, stringy cobwebs. He knew how hard the old lady had worked to make Christmas and how dismayed she'd be when she saw her tree. But he didn't blame the spiders for being curious. Instead, he decided to leave a special gift for Tante, too.

Gently, Kris Kringle touched each web. Beneath his finger, the slender strands gleamed like gold, and the dangling threads sparkled silver. Now Tante's Christmas tree was truly the most wonderful in the world.

The rooster woke Tante in the morning.

The old lady blinked in amazement at her glittering tree. "Something magical has happened!" she cried, and she climbed on her stool for a better look.

At the top of the tree, she saw one small spider finishing its web.
"Ah!" Tante nodded her head. "So it is you and your kin I have to
thank for this Christmas magic."

The little old lady understood that such wonders only happen once. Each Christmas thereafter, she did not clean so carefully but left a few webs in the rafters so that the spiders might share Christmas, too. And, every year, after she'd hung the cookies and the apples on her tree, she would nod and say, "Time for Christmas magic."

Then Tante would weave tinsel among the branches until her tree sparkled with strings of gold and silver just as it did that magical Cobweb Christmas.

AUTHOR'S NOTE

*To this day, in parts of Germany, the very first ornament
placed on the Christmas tree is a spider.*

Cobweb Christmas is based on a folktale whose roots go back more than two hundred years. Versions of this story have been told in many lands, including Germany, Poland, Russia, Romania, and Great Britain. I set this adaptation in the Bavarian forests, as this region has given us many of our Christmas tree traditions.

The word *tinsel* comes from Latin and originally meant "spark" or "flash." In the sixteenth century, thin filaments of metal were woven into fabric to add eye-catching flashes in clothing and tapestries, but it was not until the end of the nineteenth century that tinsel—originally shiny strands of brass or copper—was first included in holiday decorations. Once tinsel became a part of our Christmas trees, it also became a part of this folktale.